Brian Wildsmith
Goat's Trail

ALFRED A. KNOPF · NEW YORK

There was once a wild goat who lived high in the mountains.

"It's nice to live so near the clouds," he thought. "But I get lonely. All I ever hear are the buzz of the bees and the whistle of the wind."

One day the wind carried new sounds up from the town in the valley.

DING-DONG. HONK, HONK. VROOM, VROOM. UMP-PA-PA.

"That must be an exciting place," said the goat. "I must investigate these noises." And off he went.

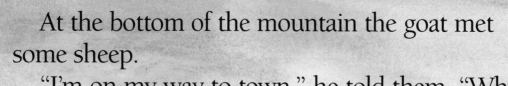

At the bottom of the mountain the goat met some sheep.

"I'm on my way to town," he told them. "Why don't you come with me?"

The sheep looked at their shepherd, who was fast asleep.

"BAA, BAA," they said.

And off they went.

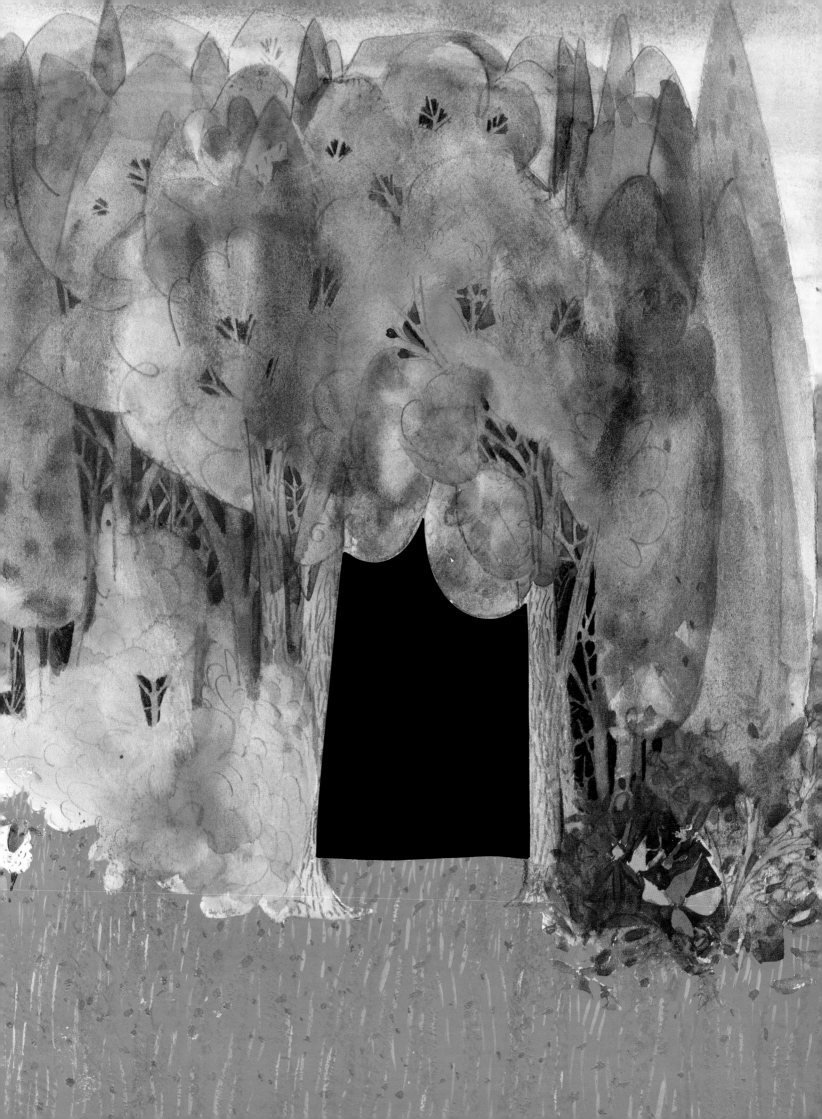

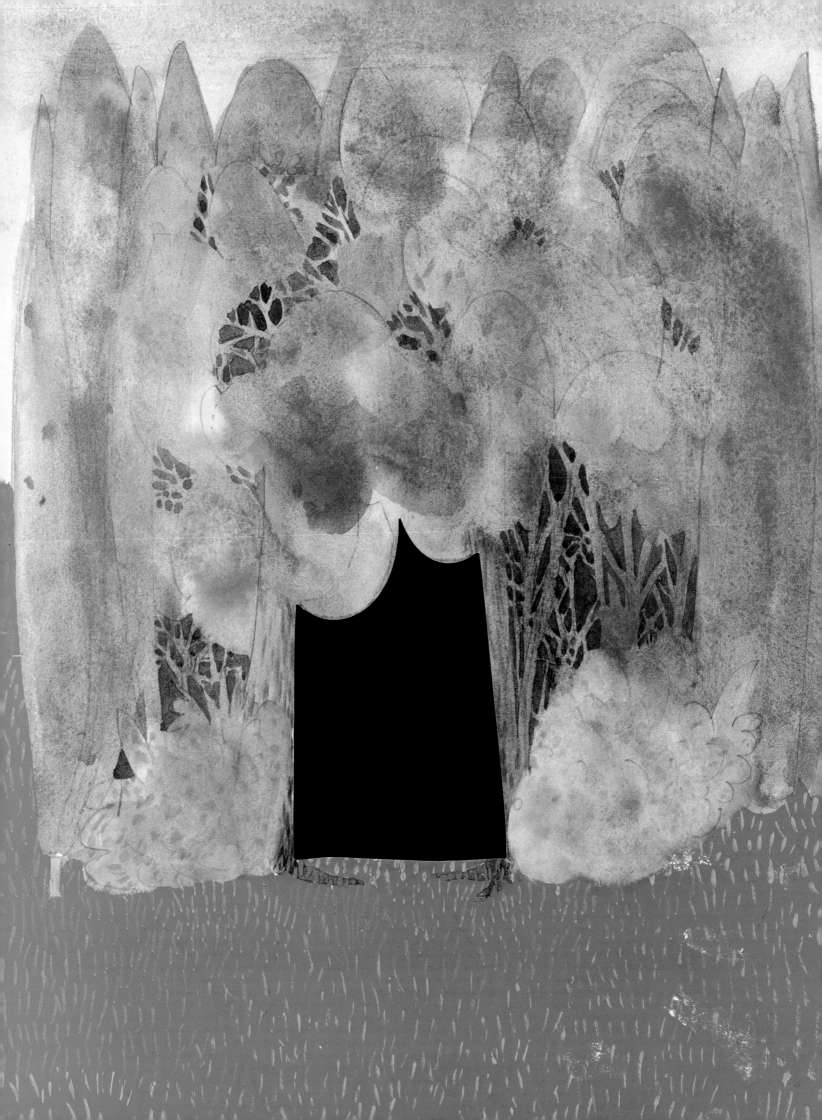

The sheep followed the goat to town.
"Listen," said the goat. And the sheep perked up
their ears to hear all the wonderful sounds.

K. VROOM, VROOM.

. "What was that?"

There was a c
"Poor cow," sa
so you can come

"MOO, MOO!" said the cow.
"BAA, BAA!" said the sheep.
"Follow me," said the goat.

On they went, listening to the wonderful sounds
of the town.

DING-DONG. HONK, HONK. VROOM, VROOM.
UMP-PA-PA...

HEE-HAW!
"What was that?" said the goat.

There stood a donkey hitched to a cart.
"Poor donkey," said the goat. "I'll set you free.
Will you give us a ride?"
"HEE-HAW," said the donkey.
They all climbed aboard and off they went.

"Follow me," said the goat.

They all ran out of the concert hall
and into the street.

Through an open doorway came some
new sounds.

"A...B...C...D...E...F...G..."

"Follow me," said the goat.

"HOORAY! HURRAH! YIPPEE!" shouted the children.
"What is the meaning of this?" said the teacher.
"The goat took my sheep," said the shepherd.
"The goat took my cow," said the farmer.
"The goat took my pig," said the swineherd.
"Stop that goat!" everyone shouted.
"Follow me," said the goat.

But this time, no one followed the goat.
And they all went home.

FOR LITTLE CARLA

This is a Borzoi Book
Published by Alfred A. Knopf, Inc.

Copyright © 1986 by Brian Wildsmith
All rights reserved under International and Pan-American Copyright
Conventions. Published in the United States by Alfred A. Knopf, Inc.,
New York, and in Great Britain by Oxford University Press, Oxford.
Distributed by Random House, Inc., New York.

Manufactured in Hong Kong
First American Edition
2   4   6   8   0   9   7   5   3   1

Library of Congress Cataloging-in-Publication Data
Wildsmith, Brian. Goat's trail.
Summary: A wild goat leads a procession of animals
into town, causing chaos and dismay. Includes die-cut
windows on each spread.
1. Toy and movable books—Specimens.
[1. Goats—Fiction. 2. Animals—Fiction.
3. Toy and movable books] I. Title.
PZ7.W647Go   1986   [E]   86-2731
ISBN 0-394-88276-8
ISBN 0-394-98276-2 (lib. bdg.)